Hot Erotica

BLACKMAILED
NANNY

SERVICING THE HELP

JACK RYDER

WARNING

This book contains sexually explicit scenes and adult language. It may be considered offensive to some readers. This book is for sale to adults ONLY.

* * * * * * * * * * * * * * * * * * *

Please store your files wisely where they cannot be accessed by underage readers.

Please feel free to send me an email. Just know that these emails are filtered by my publisher. Good news is always welcome.

Jack Ryder - **jack_ryder@awesomeauthors.org**

You might also want to check my blog for Updates and interesting info. jack-ryder.awesomeauthors.org

About the Publisher

4Fun Publishing, a member of **BLVNP Incorporated**, 340 S. Lemon #6200, Walnut CA 91789, info@blvnp.com / legal@blvnp.com
NOTE: Due to the highly emotional reaction of some people to works of erotic fiction, any email sent to the above address that contains foul language or religious references is automatically deleted by our anti-spam software and will not be seen. All other communications are welcome.

DISCLAIMER

Please don't be stupid and kill yourself. This book is a work of FICTION. Do not try any new sexual practice that you find in this book. It is fiction and not to be confused with reality. Neither the author nor the publisher or its associates assume any responsibility for any loss, injury, death or legal consequences resulting from acting on the contents in this book. Every character in this book is over 18 years of age. The author's opinions are not to be construed as the opinions of the publisher. The material in this book is for entertainment purposes ONLY. Enjoy.

The Nanny Plan
Hot Erotica

By: Jack Ryder

ISBN: 978-1-68030-052-9

Chapter One

To some people, I guess that you could say that I was born into a life of privilege; a life of financial privilege that is. Dad had made a killing at the very beginning of the computer boom of the early 90's. I was 6 years old when we moved from the suburbs of Los Angeles to our mansion north east of Seattle. Although we were not as rich as the old money millionaires from out east in the Hamptons, Dad's wealth was just beginning to amass. By the time I was ten, he was a billionaire several times over.

Even though our wealth was what you would call "new money", Mom and Dad quickly settled into the lifestyle of the rich and famous. This meant that we now had maids and butlers to take care of the mansion. We had limos with chauffeurs to take us everywhere and anywhere we wanted at anytime we wanted. My baby sister Phoebe and I even had a nanny.

Gracie was only 18 when Dad hired her to be our surrogate mother, so to speak. That was really what she was for us since Mom got so busy with her civic duties and private clubs. From the moment that Dad struck it rich; it was like our parents never again had more than a few minutes alone with us. The both of them did try to compensate for this by throwing money and gifts at Phoebe and me but Gracie who ended up becoming our only adult supervision.

At the time, I could never figure out why Gracie stayed with us all these years. From the start, Phoebe was a high maintenance child with an assortment of physical maladies and mental health issues and although I was much better equipped to take care of my own needs, I was an absolute hellion when I was a young preteen.

I constantly found little pranks to pull on Gracie. Rearranging furniture in rooms after she had set things right, adding extra soap to the laundry so it would bubble over. Rearranging things on my father's study desk after she had placed everything exactly the way he wanted them. I could only imagine what hell I put her through back then. After I reached puberty, it got even worse for her. I began peeping on her in the shower and in her bedroom when she was getting dressed.

However, by the time I reached high school, it was a little better for her. Phoebe's psychologist had finally found a combination of medications that made Phoebe much more manageable and I had let up on the pranks. Now, my main interest was finding ways to see Gracie in the nude and taking secret photos of her with either my cell phone or the fancy professional type camera that Mom had given me as a birthday gift.

I guess that you could say that I sort of had a crush on my nanny at this point. Although she was twelve years older than me, she was the prettiest woman I had ever seen. Even though I had plenty of girls at school who were willing to throw themselves at me because my father's wealth, Gracie was the only woman I ever fantasized about. She was the only girl that interested me.

With the way I treated her when I was a kid; I could not understand why she didn't simply quit. Dealing with my family was hard enough for me; I could only imagine what it was for her. I was even more shocked that Gracie stayed with us for so long after I saw exactly what my father was demanding of her. It was just after my 18th birthday and about three weeks before I was going to graduate from high school. I came home from school much earlier than usual that day and Dad happened to be home from one of his many month-long business trips.

I heard soft voices coming from the study as I came up the stairs to my room. "Yes baby...you know what I want," It was a soft moan. It was my dad's voice. As I peered around the doorframe into his open study, I saw Gracie on her knees. Her short skirt was pulled up exposing her bare ass. Her head was bobbing up and down on dad's rigid prick. Dad had his hand between her legs as he reached over her bare rump. He was fingering her pussy.

"Suck it good, baby...or I'll send those photos to your parents," he moaned. Gracie wrapped both hands around his prick and began to jerk him off while she continued to suck him. "That's it...that's it, baby," he moaned. Moments later I heard him groan loudly as he emptied himself into her mouth. "You can go now," he told her bluntly as he zipped his pants back up. I could see that she was wiping tears from her eyes as she passed by my room. My heart felt really sad for her.

I would like to tell you that I stopped peeping on Gracie after that, but I was far too enamored with her by this point in my life. I did stop taking photos of her though. And, I hid the photos that I have been taking of her for years in my laptop in an encrypted file where my father could not possibly ever access them. I also began to consider ways that I could break my father's hold on Gracie. I found myself thinking about Gracie constantly from that point on. I noticed that my fantasies about her changed too. I envisioned us being star struck lovers and that the twelve years difference in our age would not matter to her. I fantasized about doing sexual things with her that would please her and be deeply satisfying for her. I even started reading sex manuals and women's magazines in an attempt to learn how to become a terrific lover.

I noticed over the next two weeks how constantly my father fondled her whenever he thought no one would notice. There were several more times that I heard him moaning and grunting in his office. I even saw that each of the three maids was also expected to service him whenever he called them to his study. I had a knot that was beginning to grow deep in my gut. It was a huge relief when he announced that he was leaving for a five week trip to Europe.

As I saw him leaving the driveway in the limo, I had an idea pop into my head that might create an opportunity to get closer with Gracie. I really have no idea why this crossed my mind, but once I thought of it, there was a simple reasoning to it that was intriguing.

It would mean that I would have to breakup with the girl I have been dating for the last couple of months. Not a very sad loss anyway, I can't really say that she was my girlfriend. April was just a gorgeous girl from school that was willing to bang me anytime I called her. But I had made the mistake of asking her to the graduation ball. I would have to undo that. Or more precisely, make her back out.

~~***~~

April had always been pleased with our sexual arrangement. She adored having her pussy licked and was ready to give head anytime and anywhere. She seemed especially aroused any time I asked her to suck me off in public. I can't really say if my fucking skills were any good or not, but I know that she always raved about how good my 9 inch prick felt.

Pretty much, April's only off limits spot was her deliciously tight little ass. Over the couple of months that we have been banging each other, she would not even allow me to insert a finger into her anus. She would tense up tight as a drum if I even brushed a finger across her tight little pucker. The only hard part to the plan would be getting her relaxed enough to do the deed.

I took April to the drive in theater across town that Friday evening. Like so many other Friday nights, I parked my Hummer in the back row and rolled up the blacked out windows. I had her top off within moments after we got into the back seat. She has always loved having her huge puffy nipples sucked and pinched. Once I had her in the mood, I gave her a fruit drink that I had added Vodka too.

April has a tendency to get really wild and really horny when she is tipsy which is why she tends to shy away from alcohol. I put just a little bit in her first drink. But after she got used to the taste, I added more when she wasn't looking. Soon, I had her sucking my cock while I fingered her to a series of orgasms.

I had April so aroused now, that she was begging me to fuck her. "Get on your knees baby," I said it softly. "I'm gunna fuck you from behind," I reach around front to fondle her tits as I shoved my dick into her drenched pussy. April looked so sexy bent over naked in my back seat. "Give it to me, Peter...give it to me," she was wiggling her ass while my dick was slipping into her.

I grabbed her hips and fucked her savagely for nearly twenty minutes. As I pulled my dick out of her after flooding her with my seed, she was begging me for more. I smiled wickedly as I pulled my pants up and fastened them. "I'll be right back," I told her softly. "You get back in here and fuck me," she yelled as I opened the back door and got out. I saw the all four heads turn in the car parked next to us. I nodded my head to the four boys inside.

The four college boys all jumped out of the car quickly and were crawling into my Hummer within seconds. "YES...FUCK ME...FUCK ME," April moaned loudly as one of the boys mounted her. "Oh Fuck that feels good," she moaned. I slowly walked to the snack shack and bought two cups of coffee. On the way back to the hummer, I met up with the lot security man and handed him the fifty dollars we had agreed on.

"Get out of the car," he screamed into the back of my Hummer. "If the Senator finds out you are banging his daughter...." Before he could finish the sentence, all four boys flew out of the hummer and quickly left the lot in their Mercedes SUV. "April...I'm shocked that you fucked those boys while I was getting you a drink," I acted very hurt and scandalized. "If your father ever found out about this..." I let her think about that as I started the Hummer.

April was very quiet as I drove her home. I suggested that we skip the graduation ball. "If those boys are from our school, they could start rumors," I told her. "I would be so embarrassed if everyone knew what happened," I added meekly. When I dropped her off, I told her that I would call in a couple of weeks after school was out and this blew over. I think she knew I would never see her again.

~~***~~

"Oh April, I'm sorry to hear that." I was talking to my cell phone when Gracie came into the kitchen the next morning. It was turned off, but it seemed to Gracie that I was having a conversation. "Okay...I understand," I paused. "No, I won't hold that against you...I understand."

I made a grimace on my face as I pretended to hang up the phone. "That sucks," I said it very softly like I didn't know that Gracie was in the kitchen.

"What's the matter, Peter?" she whispered softly. It took all of my willpower to not gaze at her deliciously perky tits as I turned to face her. "That was April," I whispered and gazed down at the floor like I was embarrassed. "She...broke up with me." My arm tingled when she reached down to touch me gently. "It will work out okay, Peter," she said it very tenderly. "She was a bimbo anyway," she chuckled.

I quietly thanked Gracie for her support and kind words. "You have always been so kind and understanding," I told her. Then, I told her that though I was not really sad about not seeing April anymore, that I now had no date for the graduation ball. "It would be pointless to try to find a date at this late in the game," I offered.

"I have an idea," she blurted out. I had to bite my tongue to keep from screaming out my joy. I had figured that I might have to make the suggestion myself somehow. "What if...I went to the ball with you, Peter?" Again my arm tingled when she touched it. "You would...do that for me?" The sound of wonder in my voice was genuine.

"It would be my pleasure, Peter," she announced. "It will give me an excuse to dress up and be seen with the biggest hunk in all of Washington," she giggled. I felt a wiggle between my legs when she said I was a hunk. I never imagined that she might see me that way. "I would be the proudest guy in all of Washington if you will go with me, Gracie." That was absolutely the truth.

Chapter 2

I can't even describe how ecstatic I felt that Gracie offered to be my date for the ball. It was exhilarating that she considered me a hunk. When she bent over to give me a gentle kiss on the cheek, I got a terrific look down her blouse. When I saw her bare breasts underneath, I instantly got hard as a brick.

Gracie seemed a bit giddy when she stood back up. Her eyes were glued to the huge lump in my jeans. "Oh my...I need...I need...to go shower...now," she stammered. I could see a deep blush on her cheeks as she stepped back. She left the kitchen quickly and headed up to her room. I waited several moments then quietly went up to my room which is directly across from hers.

I was surprised to see her bedroom door wide open when I got upstairs. As I carefully entered her room, I could hear the sound of her glass shower door closing as she got into the shower.

I very slowly made my way to the open bathroom door. "Oh Gracie, look at you," I whispered to myself. Gracie was bent over squirting some liquid soap into her hands. My dick was painfully rigid as I gawked at her gorgeous naked body.

I pulled open the buttons on my 501 jeans and began to slowly stroke my cock right there in her room. It was the first time I had ever done that in her room. I would usually wait until she was nearly done with her shower and then race to the privacy of my room to relieve myself. It felt so nasty to be stroking myself in her room while staring at her nakedness. I was incredibly aroused.

I watched intently as her hands began to lather the soap all over her body. My dick was twitching as I watched her gently pull on one nipple and then the other. "Oooh God Yes," I gasped softly as her hand moved down between her legs. Gracie was masturbating right there...only ten feet away from me. "Oh, Fuck yes," I moaned softly as I began to ejaculate.

"PETER...WHAT ARE YOU DOING?" It was Maria, the newest and youngest maid. I had forgotten today was her day to clean the upstairs bedrooms. I quickly yanked my pants up as I glanced back at Gracie. Her eyes were riveted to my cock hanging out the front of my jeans. "I... Ugh....nothing...mind your own business," I yelled defensively. I was certain that I saw a small grin on Gracie's face as I turned to leave. "Don't ever embarrass me like that again," I scolded her.

As soon as I was in my room, I closed the door and leaned back against it. I could hear giggling coming from Gracie's room. It was at that instant that I remembered that I did not clean up the mess I made on Gracie's rug by the bathroom door. Because I got interrupted by Maria, I never got to wipe it up. I could feel my cheeks burning from my embarrassment.

~~***~~

I waited until I heard Gracie's door close and Maria going into Dad's study. I raced down the stairs and left the house without having to say anything to Gracie. My mind was in a panic as I pulled away from the estate. NOW, Gracie would never go to the ball with me. NOW, she would think of me as a pervert of some sort. I was certain that Gracie would never have anything to do with me ever again. I felt absolutely despondent.

Because classes were already out for graduating seniors, I really had nowhere to go. That's how I ended up at the mall downtown. At least I could walk off some of this nervous energy. Or at the very least, I could sit and drink coffee at the food court. When I noticed the men's clothes store, I went in to see if I could find a suit to wear in case Gracie would still go with me to the ball.

I had already decided that I did not want to wear a tux to the ball as I browsed through the suits that were hanging on the racks. After a few moments, I was joined by a distinguished looking gentleman who asked if he could help me. After a short discussion about what I was looking for, he escorted me to the back where I was custom fitted for a very nice dark grey Armani suit with a matching vest. I felt very good about the suit when I left. But I still had no idea if I would have a reason to wear it any time soon.

On the way out of the mall I happened to pass a jewelry store. In the front window, I saw an item that I instantly knew would look terrific on Gracie. If nothing else, it could be a "make up" offering. I felt more hopeful as I drove home. I was certain that Gracie would love the necklace when she saw it. I couldn't wait to see how beautiful it would look around her neck.

Gracie was out at the pool when I got home. I had nearly forgotten how sexy she is in a bikini. But this was no ordinary bikini. It had to be a new one because I would definitely have remembered seeing her in this one. It was one of those micro-bikinis. The tiny white triangles on top barely covered any of her 34C breasts and the postage stamp bottom was a thong type and the back was just a string that went into the crack of her ass.

I was really glad that she jumped into the water as I approached. I quickly sat down on the lounge chair next to hers and crossed my legs to hide the boner in my jeans. "Oooh My God," I gasped softly as she pulled herself up out of the water. The flimsy white fabric of the bikini was virtually invisible now that it was wet.

Now my dick was throbbing as I gawked at her erect nipples and the gash between her legs. "Come join me, Peter," she yelled over to me. "Oooh geezus," I groaned as she bent over to dive back in. Her bare round ass flexed as she bent her knees. I got a momentary glimpse of her pussy just as she dove forward. "I have no suit on," I yelled back.

I was very pleased that she was at least talking to me. It seemed that she was just going to act like nothing happened when she was in the shower this morning. "Just wear your underwear," she called back. As I watched her swimming across the pool, my dick was drooling pre-cum as I gazed at her bare ass. There was no way I could get in that pool with her.

"I'm sorry...but I have a phone call I need to make right now," I lied. "But I have a surprise for you when you come back in the house." I really was ecstatic that she was not mad about what had happened before I left the house. "You look...stunning...in that swimsuit," I called to her. I very quickly got up and turned my back to her so she would not see my erection. "See ya in the house," I added as I walked back to the mansion.

I could see her clearly from my bedroom window. As she laid there on the lounge by the pool, I peeped at her with my binoculars. Since her head was facing me with her on her back, she could not possibly see me. I quickly pulled my jeans down and began to jerk off as I gazed at her gorgeous body. Her wet suit did very little to block my view of her delicious round tits or her bare gash. "I want to fuck you, Gracie," I whispered to myself.

I was nearing climax when she rolled over onto her stomach. With her huge round sunglasses on, it was impossible to tell if she was looking up at me or not. But I was past the point where I could stop myself. "Oooh Fuck, Gracie," I groaned. As I stared at her bare tanned ass I shot my load all over the window sill in front of me. "Ooooh Gracie," I groaned. I noticed that she had a broad smile on her face as she got up to collect her things to come inside.

Gracie was alone in the kitchen when I came downstairs a couple of minutes later. "I wanted to say that I am sorry about this morning," I said it very quietly. "You don't have anything to be sorry about, dear." she replied. Her voice sounded happy and carefree. "Didn't you say something about a surprise?"

Even dry, her micro-bikini was so fucking sexy that it was thrilling to just look at her. She was eating ice-cream straight out of the bucket with a spoon. "You look so sexy in that," I blurted out. Gracie pulled the spoon from her mouth and licked it. I nearly shot off in my pants. "I'm glad you like it," she told me. "I bought it with you in mind," she giggled. "I'll... be right back," I groaned. I quickly turned and ran to my room to get the necklace.

"Ooooh Peeeeeeter, it's beautiful," she gasped when she opened the necklace case. The small double strand of pearls sparkled as she held them up to look at them. "That was so sweet of you, Peter." She leaned forward and kissed me twice on the cheek. "This will look wonderful with the dress I bought today for the ball," she added as she held them up again. "Such a sweetie," she sort of giggled it as she kissed me again.

I felt like I was walking on air as I left the kitchen. Gracie was NOT mad at me. She did NOT think I was some sort of pervert. AND, she was still going to the ball with me. To top it all off she had kissed me and called me a sweetie. Best of all...she loved the pearls.

With the release of all that tension, I suddenly felt exhausted. I went up to my room and collapsed on the bed. I was asleep within moments. I'm not really sure how long I was asleep, but somewhere in my conscientiousness I heard some giggling. I thought I was dreaming until I suddenly felt the glorious sensation of a hot wet mouth engulfing my prick. "Oh God," I moaned.

When I opened my eyes I was shocked to see that it was Maria that was sucking my cock. "MARIA....what the..." I had to stop to take a deep breath as she got my entire 9 inches into her throat. "Ooooh Maria," I gasped as she slowly sucked her way back up to the head. "Oooh fuck me," I moaned.

"I wanted to make it up to you for embarrassing you this morning," she whispered as she rubbed my dick back and forth across her face. She looked sexy as hell on her knees sucking my dick in her skimpy little black and white maids outfit that dad makes her wear.

I felt Maria's body begin to jerk and spasm beneath me as she felt my sperm spraying into her vagina. "Yes Peter, Oooh yes...Oooh yes," she wailed. I left my dick buried inside of her while we took a few moments to catch our breath. "Could we do this again...sometime?" She kissed the side of my neck as she asked it. "I think we could arrange that...if you really want to," I replied softly. "Oh yes, I want that very much," she giggled her reply.

Chapter 3

I was surprised to see Mom and Phoebe when I came down for dinner. They had told us that they would be leaving this afternoon on a Mom-Daughter Vacation to Paris. I could tell that Gracie was surprised too. She seemed a little sheepish about the transparent blouse that she was wearing. Although Dad insists that she wear transparent tops when he is at home, she rarely wears then when he is gone.

Mom and Phoebe seemed to be oblivious to this fact. But I noticed. The long sleeve chiffon blouse she was wearing was a bright red. Underneath, she was wearing a burgundy red transparent bra. Instead of fastening all of the buttons down the front, she had left it open but tied the bottom in a small knot just beneath her breasts. The effect was that I could see most of her bra from just above the nipples.

The skin tight jeans that she had on were those new low rider skinny jeans that sit so low on her hips that I could see the top of her thong panties which matched the burgundy bra. I had never seen Gracie dress this way before. She had also dolled herself up with makeup and put her hair back into a ponytail. I think that's because I have always told her that I love it when she wears it that way.

"I hear that you met Maria today," Mom broke through my fog. "She said it was unforgettable," she added. I saw a smile spread across Gracie's face. "Oh yes, I think they will become intimate friends," she said playfully. Although Mom and Phoebe had no clue what she meant, I had to bite my tongue to keep from laughing at her sly remark. "Yes, we seem to have connected," I replied with a smile. This time it was Gracie that had to stifle a laugh. She raised her napkin and acted like she was suppressing a cough. But I could tell that she was giggling to herself.

Mom informed us that their travel plans had changed due to a booking problem of some sort. I would later find out that it was really because her personal trainer Fernando was also going to take a vacation to Paris and that his passport had been delayed arriving in time for them to fly together unless she waited another 24 hours.

It was no secret that Mom has been banging Fernando for quite some time as well as her Pilates trainer Jorge. But this would be the first time that she so blatantly connected with either of them. Especially with Phoebe along on the trip; Phoebe would become the recipient of many lavish gifts to insure her silence on the matter.

The rest of the evening was torture for me. Gracie and I played scrabble while Mom and Phoebe chatted incessantly about their trip to Paris. I was pleased to see that Gracie's nipples were just as hard as my cock most of the evening. I also noticed that Gracie seemed to be gazing at the bulge in my sweatpants just as often as I was staring at her tits. I felt really good when I went to bed that night. Gracie was not mad my jerking off in her room. She was still going to the ball with me. She had sent Maria in to bang me. She even loved the pearl necklace that I gave to her.

Gracie gave me a very warm and very tight hug before we went up to go to bed. "I'll be thinking of you as I go to sleep," she whispered in my ear. When I crawled into bed, I reflected that this had been the best day of my life. Gracie had masturbated in front of me and seemed pleased that I had witnessed it. My dick was seeping as I began to stroke it. In my mind, I could envision her hand slipping up and down between her legs. I could see her pinching and pulling on her coral pink nipples. "Ooooh Gracie," I moaned as I shot off all over my belly. I smiled as I remembered her eyes riveted to my prick as I blew my load on her carpet.

~~***~~

It was early when I was jarred awake by the sound of voices downstairs. Phoebe was so excited by her very first trip to Europe that she was giggling and banging around as she took her luggage down stairs. I was surprised to hear Fernando's voice in the mix of chatter. It was fairly evident that Mom no longer cared about any semblance of secrecy. I could also hear Maria's voice as she volunteered to carry Phoebe's bags out to the limo.

I rolled over and drifted back to sleep. I was very disappointed to find that Gracie was gone when I finally got up. I had hoped to spy on Gracie in the shower again and even considered climbing in with her. There was a note on the kitchen table explaining that she had gone to visit her parents but assured me that she would be back on Friday in plenty of time to get ready for the ball. My heart sank with the news that I would not get to see Gracie for three whole days.

I was already beginning to worry that that maybe she was now having second thoughts about masturbating in front of me. Or maybe she felt weird that I had jizzed all over her carpet. I was lost in thought when I entered our huge 8 car garage. Smack, smack, smack, smack. "Oooh yes baby, you still have the tightest ass I have ever fucked."

I stopped in my tracks as I glanced over at the white Lincoln limo at the front of the garage. The back door of the limo was open and I could see Shelly, one of the kitchen cooks, on her knees on the side edge of the back seat. Her short skirt was up around her waist and her panties were dangling from her left foot. Joe, the chauffeur, was fucking her up the ass from behind.

"Give it to me Joe...Fuck my ass, Fuck my ass," Shelly moaned in a deep throaty voice. Joe had both hands on her hips and was pounding into her brutally. I pushed my jeans down to my knees and started to stroke myself slowly. I suddenly noticed a movement on the opposite side of the garage. It was Maria. She was standing out of sight between my Mercedes Coupe and Mom's Mercedes SUV. She was holding her skirt up with one hand and she was banging her pussy with her other hand.

"Oooh God, yes," I whispered to myself as she looked up and our eyes met. Maria smiled at me as she reached up to yank her top down to expose her tits for me. "Oooh Yesss," I moaned very softly. "OH

GOD, I LOVE YOUR TIGHT LITTLE ASS," Joe bellowed. I could tell by how fast Maria was moving her hand that she was close to orgasm. I was thrilled that her eyes were riveted to my cock as she got herself off.

"Ooooh Fuck Yes...Here it is," Joe screamed as he began to shoot his cum all over Shelly,s bare ass. I could see Maria jerking and quivering as her climax raced through her petite little body. My dick erupted three times spraying my seed all over the concrete at my feet. "Ooooh God, Yes," I moaned softly. Maria and I quickly exited the garage through opposite doors. I'm certain that Joe and Shelly were never aware that we were there.

~~***~~

I spent the afternoon running errands and making preparations for my date with Gracie. I am not sure that she would see it as a date, but in my mind this would be the most special date I had ever had. I even stopped and got my hair cut and styled. The cute little hair dresser did her best to seduce the young rich boy, but I had much more important things on my mind. I gave her a nice tip and promised I would come see her next time I need my hair styled.

Since I was the only one at home for the next several weeks, I dismissed the entire household staff. I announced that I was giving them all a two week paid vacation. Before Manfred, the butler could object, I handed him his round trip airfare to London. I knew that he has not been home to see his family in England since he came to work for my father. I could see his eyes getting a bit misty as he humbly thanked me.

Shelly was the only one who insisted to stay to prepare meals for me. She assured me that she would take her vacation as soon as the others returned. Maria seemed to have a sly smile on her face but said nothing as the others quickly collected their things and left. I was very surprised when it was Maria who brought my dinner out to me that evening. "I promised Gracie that I would take care of your needs while she is gone," Maria informed me. "ALL of your needs," she giggled.

As she was leaving, she lifted the back of her short black skirt to expose her bare ass. She was not wearing panties. "I will have another surprise for you later," she said it in a seductive sort of way. My dick was swelling quickly as she disappeared into the kitchen. I heard some whispering and giggles.

I spent the evening doing a secret chore that I had promised myself the day I saw Gracie leaving Dad's study in tears. With all of the staff gone from the estate, I would be free to search the entire property for his secret bugs and video devices. It would give me plenty of time to search his private study in an attempt to locate any photos, videos or other items that Dad was using to blackmail Gracie and the other maids with.

As a very curious young boy, I had found several secret hiding places when I was playing in his study when he was out of town. I had also found a couple of secret knobs and latches that I did not understand at that young age. I had a pretty good idea what they were for now.

I made a major discovery almost immediately when I started searching his study. The hidden latch under the bottom shelf on the right end of the bookshelf released a latch in the center of wall unit and it swung open slightly. With very little effort, I was able to swing both sides open to reveal the secret double row of shelving behind the wall unit. I found dozens of DVD cases and dozens of file folders lining the small shelves.

There were nude photographs of all of the maids including the many who had quit suddenly over the years. There were also nude photos of all the female kitchen staff members, and there were some of my mother having sex with Joe and several other men. Her current lover Fernando was one of those men. I felt a knot in my stomach as I paged through the many lurid photos.

When I pressed the secret button under the left corner of Dad's huge desk, I was able to open the very large drawer on the left side of the desk. Inside that drawer was a control panel looking device. The first switch I pushed caused the large square portrait on the opposite wall to lift up to reveal a 42 inch TV screen behind it. Each switch that I pushed after that displayed a video feed to the room that switch was for. There were also separate recording devices for each room.

I spent the next two hours reviewing all the DVDs in my room. Dad had coerced Gracie into having sex with him on the day he hired her. She had confided that she was desperate for a job because her mother was gravely ill and her family could not afford the health care she needed.

Dad told her she should strip naked if she wanted to work for him. Then he made her get on her knees to suck him. When she protested his request to take her virginity, he wrote out a check for a very large amount of money that would easily provide the health care her mother would need. "I hope your mother appreciates the sacrifice you made for her," he told Gracie glibly as he handed her the check afterwards. "As long as you do everything I tell you, she will never have to see the video I just recorded," he informed her.

All of the other videos were similar. Dad managed to manipulate each girl in his own sick way to do his bidding. The video of my Mom was more a leverage against her protests concerning his affair with his personal secretary. Once she decided to seek her own pleasure, he used that to keep her quiet about his affair and his treatment of the girls in the estate.

I felt so dirty after watching the videos that I had to take a hot shower when I was finished. I carefully made notes to where the location of the hidden cameras might be based on the angles of the photo feed on the recordings. I was just completing that when there was a soft knock on the door. "Can I come in?" Maria whispered as she cracked my door open. When I saw how she was dressed, there was no way I would say no.

Chapter 4

Maria was wearing a white transparent baby doll nightie without panties. Her dark brown shin looked marvelous through the flimsy white fabric. I could clearly see her pointy cone shaped tits and her dark brown nipples looked like chocolate drops that would melt in your mouth. My dick was quickly swelling in my jeans.

"I have a surprise for you, Peter," she said coyly as she stepped forward into the room. Just behind her, Shelly stepped into the doorway. "Oooh Geezus," I moaned. Shelly was wearing one of those bright pink mini dresses that is made entirely of mesh which makes it transparent too. Because she was nude underneath, I could see every inch of her creamy white body. My dick was completely erect now. Her short red hair looked lovely against the bright pink outfit.

"Did you enjoy the show this morning?" Shelly said it softly as she stepped behind Maria. "Yes, but not nearly as much as this one." You could hear the arousal in my voice as Shelly pulled Maria's top down and began to pinch and pull on Maria's nipples from behind. "Isn't she pretty?" Shelly whispered as she kissed the side of Maria's neck. "Oooh god...you are both...so damn sexy," I gasped softly.

"I hope you have no plans for tomorrow," Maria giggled. "We are going to take turns fucking you all night," she added with a playful wink. For the next several moments I just sat there and watched them kissing and fondling one another. My dick was seeping fluid into the crotch of my jeans. I could not remember ever being this excited and aroused. "You can have him first," Maria announced when they ended a very long French kiss. "I've already got to have him once," she told Shelly as a matter of fact while she patted her on the rump.

They came to the bed and began to undress me together. They each untied a shoe and yanked it off with the sock. Then they unfastened my jeans and each grabbed a leg to pull on till they had my pants off. As Maria pulled my tank top over my head, Shelly gave my bikini brief underwear a very hard tug and literally ripped them off of me. "Look at thaaaaat," she giggled joyfully as she saw my rigid 9 inch prick spring free. "I told you," Maria laughed.

"Oooooh God, Yesssss," I groaned loudly as Shelly bent forward and took my manhood into her drooling mouth. Maria scooted forward and began to kiss me very passionately. This was so amazing for me. I had never kissed a girl while another was sucking my cock. "Uuummmm," I moaned into Maria's mouth. Gluck, Gluck, Gluck...Shelly made gagging sounds as she forced more and more of my dick into her throat.

Maria sat up and pulled her nightie off and told Shelly to let me scoot down so my head would be flat on the bed. As Maria moved on top to straddle my face, Shelly scooted up and guided my dick to her dripping gash. "Ooooh God, he's huge," she moaned when I was about 6 inches inside of her. My three inch girth was stretching her as she very slowly pressed down till I was completely buried inside. I could feel her whole body trembling as she just sat there impaled on me. "Isn't he delicious?" Maria whispered.

The sensation of Maria's pussy grinding on my mouth as Shelly humped back and forth on my prick was spectacular. Watching them kissing and fondling each other as they fucked together had my cock so hard that I thought I would burst any moment. The syrupy fluid that was oozing into my mouth from Maria's gash was like a sweet warm nectar. "Yesssss, Peter, Yesss," she moaned as I swirled my tongue around her engorged clit.

Shelly and Maria had let go of each other and were both savagely grinding on me faster and harder. I could tell that Maria was building up for her climax so I reached my right hand between her legs and shoved two fingers deep into her pussy. "Oooh Yes, Peter...Yes," she bellowed. As I drilled my fingers in and out of her, I lapped forcefully on her clit. That sent her over the edge.

"Oh My God Yes...Oh My God Yes," she screamed. A huge flood of her nectar gushed into my mouth as she got off. "Ooooh Peter," she moaned as her body quivered.

After Maria rolled off my face onto her back, I twirled Shelly over onto her back and shoved her legs back till her feet were next to her head. "Ooooh yes, Peter...Fuck Me...Fuck Me," Shelly moaned. It was a very deep primal sort of utterance. Smack, smack, smack...As I pounded into Shelly, Maria propped herself up on an elbow to watch me fucking this beautiful petite little redhead.

"FUCK ME...FUCK ME...FUCK ME," Shelly screamed. I could feel her beginning to vibrate underneath me. "Give it to her Peter...Fill her with your seed," Maria whispered. Shelly was jerking and flailing beneath me as my cock began to spew my seed deep into her womb. "Oooh My God Yes...Oooh Yes...Oooh Yes." It felt like my entire body was in a spasm as my cock erupted again and again. "Oooh Peter, Yes...Yesssss," Shelly moaned.

As we rested for a while the girls petted me tenderly and nibbled on my neck. It was all like some thrilling dream as each of them would bend down for a moment to lick and suck on one of my nipples. Then the other would do the same to the other nipple. They were also gently fondling my testicles and petting my prick. "This must be for me," Maria chuckled playfully when my cock sprang back to full erection.

This time, Shelly just laid next to us and held Maria's hand while I pounded into Maria over and over. It was electrifying for me when she reached over and began to gently pet my ass. As I continued to rut into Maria, Shelly scooted over and was kissing on my body and letting her hand wander all over my ass and inner thighs.

Maria wrapped her legs up around my waist and was humping herself up to meet my every thrust. "Fuck Me Peter, Fuck Me," she grunted. The sensation of her fingernails digging into my back as Shelly began to rub her finger against my anus was exquisite. "OOOOH YES, PETER, I'M CUMMING...I'M CUMMING," she screamed. As Maria started to twitch and convulse beneath me, Shelly shoved her finger into my ass. "OH MY GOD YES...FUCK YES, FUCK YES." My cock exploded so forcefully that it felt like every particle of semen that was stored in my sack flooded out in one gigantic gush as my body jerked uncontrollably. "Ooooh....Fuck Me," I panted weakly as I rolled off of Maria. "That...was...spectacular," I panted.

The girls both crawled up on either side of me and petted me gently and kissed my chest very tenderly. "Yes, we will fuck you a lot more," Maria giggled. "But I think you've had enough for one night." She lifted her head and kissed me on the cheek as I continued to gasp for air. They were both curled up against me as I drifted off to sleep. "I'm the luckiest guy on Earth," drifted through my mind as I fell asleep.

I heard them in the shower giggling when I woke up. With the bathroom door wide open, I could easily see both of them playing with each other in the shower. "Oooh Yes, Shelly," Maria gasped when Shelly got on her knees and shoved her face between Maria's legs. I rested on an elbow and watched as Shelly hungrily ate Maria out. It was such a pleasure to just lay there and see these two petite women having sex with each other.

I had to admit to myself that Dad had a very definite taste in women. It had never occurred to me until now that all of the girls he has hired over the years are young and very petite. As I gazed at them in the shower, it was obvious that they have an identical body type. These girls were very petite with perky cone shaped breasts; they are both five foot two.

But that is where the similarity ends. Maria is very dark brown with waist length silky black hair. Her eyes look like black opals. Her nipples look like delicious drops of chocolate. Shelly is a very creamy white skinned redhead. Her amber red hair is mid length and wavy. Her eyes are like sparkling green emeralds. Her coral pink nipples are very puffy and beg to be nibbled on.

As I think back, I remember that Gracie was a very slender and petite 5 foot 6 when Dad hired her twelve years ago. But as time passed she has developed into a gorgeous bombshell. Her figure has grown into a very shapely 34C-22-34. Her breasts are perfectly round like grapefruit with large flat pink areolas and nipples that look like pencil erasers. Although playing with these young petite girls has been spectacular, it is the shapely womanhood of Gracie that I desire and crave beyond all reason.

As I watched Shelly and Maria get each other off in the shower, I decided that I should tell them about my discovery of Dad's DVDs and his blackmailing deeds. I thought that they should know that I am aware of their situation with him. I wanted them to know that I am trying to figure out a way to end his manipulative hold on them. As I saw them drying off in the bathroom, I patted the bed next to me. "Come sit down, there's something we need to discuss," I called to them.

Shelly sat to my left and Maria was on the right. Although they both had bath towels wrapped around them, the towels spread open when they sat down and I could see all the way down to their bare gashes. Although I wanted to rip their towels off and have them both, I needed to get this out of the way. "There's something I need to tell you both," I whispered softly as I gawked at their bare cunts.

After I spent the next ten minutes revealing the discoveries I made in dad's study and how I had watched each of his DVDs, there was a momentary silence. I was not exactly sure what either of them were thinking at that moment, but I noticed that they both had a sheepish sort of grin on their face. Maria was the one who made the confession.

"We have a plan too," she announced softly as her hand came over to pet my right thigh. "Shelly and I planned to get pregnant by you and then tell your dad that he knocked us up," Maria lifted her eyes to peer directly into mine. "But we only had sex with you because we really wanted to be with you," she added. "I have fantasized about you for two years," Shelly blurted out.

Although I was surprised by their confession, I was not angry about it in the least. I was flattered that they had both really wanted me and it aroused me that they both wanted me to impregnate them. "We better get started then," I laughed playfully. As I stood up, I could see a joyous relief spread across their faces. "But first, there is something we need to do," I told them. "It will make it unnecessary for him to consider a DNA test.

I took the girls to the study and showed them where his hidden equipment was. Then, I erased the video of Shelly fucking Joe in the garage while Maria and I watched. She was thrilled to see us masturbating when we watched her. Then I erased the video of me searching dad's study including the present invasion into his private equipment. After I had the girls leave the room, I added a ten second delay so I could exit with being recorded. The game was now in progress.

I decided that accusing dad of being the father might be too risky. When I called the three girls that had quit abruptly over the last several years, I found that each of them had gotten pregnant by him and he had given each of them one million dollars to go away. His reasoning was that he was supporting each of his children from the past maids with 50K per year until they turn twenty. In return, the women were not to disclose their sexual relationship or who the father was. They were forbidden to talk with any journalists for any reason.

I knew that the only thing my father likes as much as his money, is keeping his secrets intact. I was fairly certain that he would agree to hush up any apparent indiscretion that involved his son knocking up his hired help. My plan would make it vividly obvious who the father was for Shelly and Maria's pregnancies. It would also be a slap in his face that I apparently seduced his two favorite girls away from him.

The girls were thrilled with my plan. They were especially happy that we would have so much fun carrying it out. And even better, that dad would have to witness me impregnating them. The only reservation I felt inside was that I feared this might cost me any hope of having a relationship with

Gracie. After the deed was done and both girls were pregnant, Gracie might lose interest in whatever novel fantasy she might have had for me. But deep inside, I felt that I was doing the right thing. I could not just sit back and let my dad use these girls for his own gratification. All the other girls had told me that they welcomed his attention and willingly played his sexual games. But he had crossed the line with Gracie, Shelly and Maria.

I took Maria out to the garage after breakfast while Shelly acted like she was doing her normal daily chores in the kitchen. I slowly stripped Maria naked right in front of where I knew the hidden camera was and then I led her to dads white limo and had her lay across the back seat with her legs sticking out the back door. "Yes Peter....Fuck me...Fuck me," she bellowed as I stepped between her legs and mounted her.

I knew that from this angle, dad would clearly see my dick slamming in and out of Maria's gash. I have to admit that I got a perverse sense of pleasure knowing that he would have to watch me fucking his favorite new girl. That he would know that I had filled her with my seed and knocked her up. "Give it to me Peter, Give it to me...Give it to me," Maria screamed lustfully.

"Here it is baby...here it is...here it is," I yelled my reply. My legs vibrated and my body jerked each of the four times that my dick erupted inside of Maria's sex. I could feel her vaginal muscles spasm and grip my cock each time my seed sprayed into her. "Oh Peter, yes...yes, yesssss," she moaned. I was pleased to see that a bit of my mess oozed out onto the seat when I yanked my dick out of Maria. I made sure to leave it right there for dad to see.

I left Maria in the garage to get dressed and went into the house. I did not look at Shelly or say a word to her as I crossed through the kitchen. As soon as I was in the hallway leading to the guest rooms and staff quarters, I turned to face Shelly and blew her a kiss. In the hallway, dad's hidden cameras could not see me. I held up two fingers and winked at her. That was the signal for her to meet me in her quarters after lunch.

I fucked Shelly in her bed just beneath dad's camera after lunch that day. Then I fucked them both on the couch in the family room that evening. Although there was no camera in my room when I fucked them both again before we slept together, I was pleased that I had filled them both three times that day with my baby milk. And four of those hookups would be seen by my father.

I fucked Maria in dads study the next day and then did Shelly out in the cabana by the pool in the afternoon. In the evening we all screwed each other in the downstairs gym where dad had made the video of Mom having sex with Fernando. I again fucked both of them in my bed before we slept. In a little over two days, I had filled them both with my seed eight times. I can't begin to describe how thrilling all of this was for me.

We were all exhausted by the time we fell asleep that Thursday night. But it was a wonderfully satisfying tiredness for all of us. Over the last three days, we had enjoyed every moment of each day. We had reveled in the torrid sexual hookups; we had played and giggled while we prepared for each of the recorded sex romps. We had loved the intimacy we felt when we fell asleep each night. There was a common bond between the three of us that was even deeper than the sexual bond. A that bond would grow stronger when the children are born.

Chapter 5

The girls had already left when I got up Friday morning. Actually, it was near noon when I crawled out of the bed. I slept over ten hours that night. The exhaustion finally took over and I slept more soundly than I could ever remember. After I took a much needed pee, I climbed into the shower and just stood there for a long time. The hot water felt delicious as it soothed the tight muscles and invigorated me.

I was stunned when I opened the shower door after I finished washing. Gracie was sitting against the sink counter and she was smiling at me as I stood there completely naked in front of her. She handed me a towel and then sat against the counter again. "Nice to see you, Peter," she giggled. At that moment, I was deeply worried about how Gracie was going to respond to the likelihood that I will have babies with Shelly and Maria.

My eyes poured over her lovely body as I dried myself off in front of her. She was wearing a short tan skirt and I could see her creamy thighs as she sat there on the counter. Her sleeveless white blouse was transparent enough that I could see her lacy push up bra pressing her tits together and making them look even more delicious to me. It was unbuttoned all the way to just below her bra. Her sapphire blue eyes seem to peer into my soul as she sat there grinning at me.

"I hear you've been very busy the last three days," she said coyly. "Gracie, I can explain...it was." Gracie stood up and placed her finger against my mouth before I could finish. "Don't be silly," she laughed. "I was the one that arranged for them to stay with you," she reminded me. "I sent them home till Monday," she informed me as she turned to leave.

Every fiber of my being wanted to run to her and rip that skirt off so I could fuck her right there in the doorway. My dick was throbbing against my stomach as she turned back to face me. "I am looking forward to our date tonight, Peter." Her eyes glanced down to my engorged prick. "I'll be ready by 7pm," she added softly. She winked playfully as she walked out. "Oh God," I moaned.

I was ecstatic as I made my preparations that day. Gracie had called our evening plans a date. She seemed to have enjoyed gawking at me while I was naked. I had noticed that her nipples got rock hard when she stared at my rigid manhood. Although I was still uncertain how she would feel about me making babies with the girls, I was beginning to think it might not matter to her.

I called and confirmed our dinner reservations. I again had my hair styled. And I took my car in to be cleaned and waxed. I picked up my new Armani suit from the clothier and then went to purchase a new pair of black dress shoes. On the way out of the mall, I stopped in that jewelry shop again and bought a pair of white pearl cufflinks for my dress shirt. I thought it might be a nice touch to have pearls that matched Gracie's necklace.

I felt incredibly giddy as I drove home to start getting ready. I have had many dates in my teen years and have bedded more than my fair share of them. But none of them ever mattered to me like this. None of them had ever been more than a curious adventure for me. The excitement that I was feeling now was wonderfully overwhelming.

Gracie looked radiant as she came down the stairs at 7pm. She was wearing a long strapless sapphire blue evening dress that was slit up one side all the way to her hip. The strapless top of the dress had bra cups sewn in that pushed her breasts together and made them bulge at the top edge of the dress. Her light golden hair had large billowy curls that framed her face. There was were two strands that had been braided to wrap around and tie behind her head to hold the rest of her beautiful hair hanging down the middle of her back down to her waist.

"You look wonderful, Peter," she broke my stunned silence as she glanced up and down my body. The dark grey Armani suit did look very nice and the coal black shirt was a good choice as well. "You look...breathtaking," I gasped my reply. The white shiny pearls around her neck were even more beautiful than I had imagined. My dick was fully erect by the time I climbed into the driver's seat of my Mercedes coupe.

Since the slit in dress was on the left side, I was able to see her entire left leg all the way up to her hip as she sat there in the passenger seat. It was obvious that she was not wearing any panties. It took every bit of my concentration to not gawk at her as I drove us to dinner. It took even more restraint in the restaurant as many of the men gazed at her lustfully while we chatted and enjoyed our meal together.

"I never knew you could be such a perfect gentleman," Gracie told me when we were both back in the car. "While every man in there undressed me with their eyes, you paid attention to ME." She reached over and laid her hand on my thigh. "We are going to have a wonderful journey," she whispered. Although I had no idea what she meant about a journey, I was very pleased that she had said...WE.

It almost felt like time stopped as Gracie and I entered the ballroom in the downtown convention center. Although the music was still playing and there were couples dancing out on the dance floor, everyone turned towards us as we walked in arm in arm. Gracie had her right arm wrapped around my left arm and her right hand was resting on my bicep. I slowly walked her over to a vacant table near the back wall and pulled a chair out for her to sit in. "Oooh geezus," one of the young fellas near our table gasped when Gracie kissed my cheek before she sat down.

I did my very best to continue to pay attention to Gracie while we chatted and waited for a slow dance to be played. But I have to confess that I was bursting with pride as I noticed so many of the young men in the hall staring at Gracie with such obvious lust. Gracie was by far the most beautiful woman in the room. Although most of the college age girls were very pretty, Gracie had that womanly voluptuous beauty that most men dream of.

When the long awaited music finally played and I guided her to the dance floor, I felt like we were floating on a cloud as I held her in my arms while we danced. I hardly was aware that there was anyone else in the building. It felt like heaven was holding me in her arms.

The feeling of her breasts mashing against my chest felt divine. I felt her free hand wander up and down my back as I pulled her close and let my hand fall to just above her rear end. I hesitated there afraid that it might offend her if I fondled her ass.

"It's okay, Peter...I want you to touch me," she whispered it in my ear and then kissed the side of my neck. "Oooh God," I moaned softly as she kissed me a second time and allowed her free hand to squeeze my ass. I moved my hand down and began to gently fondle her soft round ass.

"Yesssss, baby," she whispered. I felt her hips press forward and she was rubbing against the bulge in my pants.

By the third time we danced, we were both touching and fondling each other rather openly. "Let's get out of here...I have a surprise for you," she whispered. I was very happy with the suggestion as my cock was beginning to seep pre-cum from all of our petting. There were many eyes following us as we left the ballroom holding hands. It thrilled me how her left leg was bared with each stride of her left foot. Her long bare sleek leg looked so sensuous.

When we got out to the car, Gracie told me that she would need to drive. "It's all part of the surprise," she told me as I held the door open for her to get in. As we pulled on to I-90 east,

I decided to tell her about the girls wanting me to get them pregnant. "I have something I need to tell you Gracie, I hope it won't change how you feel about me," I told her softly.

After I told her exactly what the girls wanted from me and exactly what we had been doing to make it happen, Gracie glanced over and smiled at me sweetly. "I know all about that, Peter," she told me softly. "I was the one who gave them the idea." Her eyes locked onto mine for a few seconds then returned to the road.

I was quiet for several moments as I considered her words. "So...is that what THIS is all about?"

I was starting to feel a knot in my gut. "You want me to knock you up so you can get even with my dad?" I was beginning to feel like a very foolish young man who had been manipulated. I was beginning to feel like the entire last four days had been an elaborate plan to use me as a weapon against my shithead father. "Is that it? I was just a dumb kid that the three of you could easily use to even the score?"

Gracie glanced over at me. There seemed to be tears in her eyes and pain on her face. She quickly pulled the car over on to the truck chain up area at the side of the road. "It's not like that Peter," she said softly as she shut off the ignition. "I admit that I wanted to help Shelly and Maria but we have no intentions of hurting you in any way." She reached over and laid her hand on my arm. "We all adore you, Peter."

I could feel her hand trembling as it rested on my arm. "I don't need anything from you to be free from your father," she whispered. "My father died five years ago and my Mom passed away six months ago...he has no hold on me now." I lifted my head to look her in the eyes. "Then why did you stay?" I asked. "Because I want you Peter...I want...you." She pulled her hand back to wipe a tear from her cheek. "I was hoping...that you...would want me too," she whispered it.

I unhooked my seatbelt and leaned over to her. I pulled her to me and kissed her very passionately. I could hear her moaning into my mouth. "Yes Gracie...I want you too," I gasped.

I had no idea where Gracie was taking us as she pulled off the expressway in the North Bend area. We drove up into the foothills and we ended up at a very nice log cabin looking dwelling that was alone by the edge of the forest. "This was my mother's home; she left it to me in her will." Gracie announced it as she unlocked the door. "I spent the last three days getting this ready for tonight...this is my surprise."

As soon as the door was closed behind us, Gracie pressed me against the wall with her body and brought her hands up to my face. "Kiss me again, Peter, like you did in the car." I could hear a deep lust in her voice. Gracie craned her head up and we kissed for several minutes. It was as if we tasted each other. Exploring and experimenting with our lips and our tongues. My hands wandered down to fondle her lovely ass. Then I brought them up to her breasts. "Yesss, baby, Yesss," she moaned into my mouth as I felt her tits for the very first time.

Gracie suddenly stepped back. I was amazed as I watched her reach up and begin to unzip her evening dress. The zipper was on the side of the dress where the slit at the bottom was. As she pulled the zipper down, the very tight dress fell away from her body until it fell off onto the floor by her feet. She was now completely nude except for her white pearls and 3 inch heels.

"Do you think I'm pretty?" She said it so softly I could barely hear it. "Ooooh Gracie, you are so beautiful," I gasped softly. My hands instinctively rose to gently fondle her breasts. Although I have seen her naked so many times before, this was my dream come true. She was inches away from me and I could touch her. She wanting me to touch her, she was exposing herself to me openly. "Sooooo beautiful," I moaned as her nipples became rigid while I fondled her.

"Could you ever...love someone...so much older?" Her voice sounded almost timid. "Oh Gracie, I already love you. I have always loved you," I blurted out. I pulled her forward and kissed her very roughly as my hands wandered all over her naked body. "I have always wanted you, Gracie, always." My entire body was trembling with arousal as I scooped her up into my arms. I heard two clunks on the floor as her heels fell off.

"Then, I am all yours, if you'll have me," she whispered into my ear.

Gracie wrapped her arms around my neck as I carried her into the family room. I gently sat her in the center of the couch pit and slowly began to strip myself for her. "It's about time that I get to watch you undress," she giggled. "Since you have been watching me all these years," she taunted. The fact that she has known that I have been watching her just made my dick even harder.

"So, you were putting on a show for me," I teased back. "Did it make your pussy wet when I jerked off for you?" I chided. Gracie was now rubbing her gash as I kicked off my shoes and started to pull my pants down. "Oooh God, yes...it did," she moaned as she watched my cock spring out of my shorts. Her eyes were riveted to my throbbing 9 inch prick as I kicked my shorts off onto the floor. "See something you like, baby?" I taunted. "FUCK ME PETER... please don't make me wait another moment," she gasped loudly

I got on my knees between her legs and pulled her forward till her pussy was right at the edge of the couch. I very slowly pressed the head of my prick into her. "Give it to me Peter; I want it all," she moaned." I very slowing pressed forward and watched as each inched disappeared into her dripping gash. There are no words to describe how thrilling it felt to see my dick sliding into this gorgeous woman that I have admired and lusted over for so many years. "Oh Gracie," I moaned in a deep husky voice.

The expression on Gracie's face as I began to hump in and out of her told me that she has lusted for this too. It was a look of total bliss and satisfaction. I reached forward and rolled her nipples between my fingers. "Yesssss, Yesssss," she purred as she arched her back to jut her tits out even further. I bent forward and started to suck hungrily on one tit and then the other as I continued to hump into her willing sex hole. "Oooh Peter...Oooh Peter," she gasped softly.

When I felt her body starting to vibrate as her first orgasm flood-ed through her, I moved back up and twisted on both of her nipples while I held my dick buried to the root. "Oooh Peter, Yesss, Yesssss, Yesssss, she screamed while her body twisted and jerked beneath me. I could feel her pussy contract with each spasm and it was the most exquisite sensation I had ever felt.

"Ooooooh Peeeeeeter," she moaned in a throaty voice as she finally relaxed beneath me. I quickly pulled my dick out and had her get on her knees at the edge of the couch. "Take me Peter, Take me," she moaned when I slammed my dick into her from behind. Smack, smack, smack, smack. My belly slapped against her luscious ass with each savage thrust into her drenched pussy.

I held tightly to her hips as I pounded into her and remembered every night I had laid in bed and jerked off...dreaming of this moment. "Oooh Gracie, Oooh Gracie," I grunted. Smack, smack, smack, smack. I could feel the sperm boiling up in my nut sack as I rammed as far into her as I could manage. "Give it to me Peter...fill me up, baby," she bellowed. I could feel her convulsing into another orgasm as I shoved all the way inside and exploded. "Oh my God, yes...oooh yes, oooh yes," I screamed my reply.

My legs jerked and vibrated as I held myself buried in her. My dick sprayed four huge ropes of my sticky white seed deep into her quivering womb. "Oh My God, Gracie...Oh My God," I moaned. I left myself buried in her for several long moments after I stopped cumming. I wanted to always remember this moment forever. Gracie was gazing back at me with a huge smile as I stared at her gorgeous naked body. It felt so fucking good to be inside of her after all these years that I hated to pull away from her.

"It's okay baby, we can do this again...any time you like," she whispered. There was no longer any doubt in my mind that Gracie truly did want me. The loving expression on her face conveyed that she has waited for this moment too. That she is just as thrilled that we finally got to make our fantasy come true. "That was sensational, Peter." My cock slipped out just as she said it. We both lied down together on the bed catching our breath.

Epilogue

Gracie and I spent the entire weekend screwing our brains out that first time together. Gracie confided that she had realized that she'd fallen in love with me a couple of years ago but had tried to ignore her feelings until she was certain that I might feel the same way about her.

When she gave me a tour of the split level home on that Saturday morning, I noticed that the one of the rooms between the two upper level bedrooms was vacant. "That room is going to be the nursery," she informed me with a chuckle. My mind was reeling as she led me to the kitchen in the lower level of the house.

After handing me a cup of coffee, we sat at the kitchen table and she told me the rest of the surprise. She informed me that she had called my father and quit her job on Monday; the day that Mom and Phoebe left for vacation. Then, she told me that Shelly and Maria had both called him that day and quit too. "You see, none of us wanted to hurt you," she added. "We ALL just want YOU."

After our conversation, she showed me where their bedrooms would be. Apparently, Shelly and Maria were going to live with us and raise my children here. We would all live together like a family. I called my father that day and informed him that I had found his DVDs and that I would be moving out with the women who had quit. After some harsh words and denials, I convinced him that he should support my two children in the same manner as his three illegitimate kids.

I never thought things would end up this way. For some people, these things would never happen in their lifetime and I got to experience all of them. I have always felt that it is a magical thing when you can find someone in your life that WANTS you more than anything on Earth. It is incredible to me that I have found three women in my life that feel that way about me. I guess for some people, they could say that I'm the luckiest son of a bitch in the world.

The End

Here is a preview of another story you may also enjoy:

JACK RYDER

HOT EROTICA

TAKE
THREE
MR. WRITER

I was in no hurry that second Monday in April as I made the early afternoon drive from my cabin home in Woodinville south to Seattle. It was a moderate day temperature wise with lots of sun breaking through the high white billowy clouds. Some people in this area call those sun breaks.

But I prefer the idea of mostly sunny skies.

I was quite amazed when the local university had invited me to conduct their two-week spring break writer's symposium and clinic for young aspiring authors. I was awarded an Honorary Professorship to add to my list of credentials. It amused me as I was drawing near Seattle that most of those REAL professors would probably have a coronary if they knew that nearly half of my income came from writing erotic romances. Books that most of them would consider literary pornography.

As I was pulling into the parking garage, I prefer to park my own car so I know where it's at when I want to make private late night adventures around the area. I felt a certain curiosity as to WHY any young college age student would waste their two week spring break to hang out with some old 42 year writer who had dropped out of college one full year before completing his degree.

I saw the three young girls as I pulled into a parking spot near the back of the parking garage. The tallest girl, who was obviously the oldest of the three was bent over with her ass hanging out the back of their Subaru Wagon. Her short skirt had hiked up so far that I could easily see her lacy boy-shorts style panties wedged into the crack of her ass. The other two girls were just standing there next to her laughing.

I parked my huge black Hummer a couple of spaces away then made my way over to see if I could be of assistance. It was a large luggage case that was caught on the rear passenger's seat belt. Because it was very heavy, the young girl could not wrestle it free. "Could I give you a hand with that Miss?" I asked softly. "Damn thing's stuck," she grumbled as she stepped back and stood up.

I tried to keep from looking down since her skirt was still hiked up. I kept my eyes glued to hers as she reached down and wiggled the skirt down to cover her exposed crotch. "Hoping for a free peep show?" she groused softly. "No, I just thought I could be of assistance." I continued to stare into her shockingly radiant blue eyes. "I can leave if you prefer," I smiled as I began to turn away.

"NO...I could...use some help," she whispered. I smiled as I felt her hand touch my arm.

After I managed to get the stuck bag out of the car, I pulled out all the rest of their luggage and stacked it neatly on the garage floor. Before they could say anything, I was on my cell phone.

"Yes...I have a reservation for room 919. Could you send a luggage trolley out to the parking garage...stall 23E." That was the stall that the Subaru was parked in. "There will be someone out to assist you momentarily," I told the girls as I started to walk away with my luggage in hand.

"Gee, that was really nice." One of the girls whispered. "Nice to see that there are still some gentlemen left in the world," I recognized the oldest girl's voice reply. "Gee, it's too bad he's so old," the third girl giggled. I sort of grimaced as I continued on. "I think older men can be quite sexy," I heard the older girl's voice again just before I moved out of earshot. I could hear the other two girls giggling softly.

I saw the three girls checking in as I got onto the elevator with my luggage. I told the bell hop that I preferred to carry my own bags because I keep my laptop and story notes packed inside. As I pressed button number 9, I saw the older girl running towards the elevator. Her waist length coal black hair swishing back and forth. I tried to hit the hold button but it was too late. The door closed between us. But not before I noticed that she had opened the top three buttons on her blouse. Not before I got a terrific view of the top of her 36C melons.

I quickly unpacked my luggage once I was in my room. Because I got here plenty early, I would have plenty of time to relax before the scheduled dinner in the main ballroom followed by my welcoming speech for the symposium. I filled the Jacuzzi in my private suite and stripped naked.

Although I brought a swimsuit with me, I didn't bother to put it on since I was alone in my suite.

I called the front desk and requested a bottle of brandy be sent up and slipped into the hot bubbling water of the Jacuzzi.

There was a knock on my door about five minutes later. I quickly grabbed a bath towel to wrap around my waist and a $20 bill to tip the bell hop. "I wanted to apologize for my rudeness." It was the girl with the black hair and big tits again. It was a bit awkward standing there with just a towel and her mouth gaping open. "Yeah, an old fart like me could have been some sort of pervert," I teased her.

She blushed as she lowered her head for a moment. I was pleased to get another quick look down her blouse as she collected her thoughts. "I'm sorry about that too," she whispered. "We were all very rude to you." She lifted her head to look into my eyes. "You certainly don't look like an old man to me," she whispered as she glanced up and down my dripping wet muscular body.

"Yeah...but the jury is still out on the pervert thing," I quipped with a smile.

The sound of her giggle was wonderful. "Your apology is accepted, Miss?" She reached out like she wanted to shake my hand. "Chloe...my name is Chloe," she announced. "My name is Jake,"

I answered her. "I'd take your hand...but then the question of my being a pervert might take a turn for the worse," I chuckled as I glanced down at my hands clutching the towel around my waist. Again, she giggled. Then she bent forward and kissed me on the cheek. I got one more terrific glance at her yummy firm tits. "You're really sweet," she told me as she backed away. "I hope to talk to you again," she added as she turned to leave.

The bellhop was just coming up the hallway as Chloe made her way to the elevator. So I got to watch her yummy round ass swishing back and forth all the way there. I felt a little wiggle as she turned to wave at me. The grin on her face suggested that she enjoyed knowing that I had gawked at her all the way down the hall. I handed the $20 to the bellhop just as she stepped on to the elevator. It tickled me when she poked her head back out and puckered up to blow me a kiss.

I quickly closed my door as my cock began to swell. It just wouldn't be cool to start sporting wood with the bellhop still glaring at me. I put the brandy on the counter in the suite kitchen then went to drain the water from the Jacuzzi. I decided that now would be a good time to take that nap I planned on so I would be fresh for the evening festivities.

I tried to ignore the boner that was throbbing between my legs when I first laid down for my nap.

But my mind kept recalling Chloe bent over the back of the Subaru with her luscious ass fully exposed…

To purchase this book, look for **Take Three, Mr. Writer.**

Here is another preview of a story you may enjoy:

SHYLA STARR

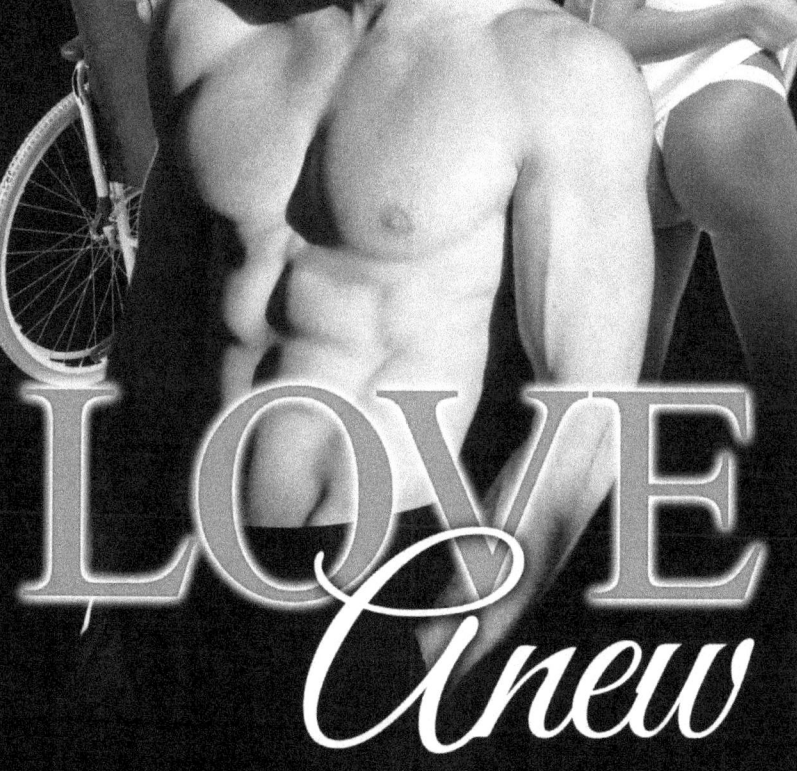

LOVE
Anew

LONELY BILLIONAIRE ROMANCE SERIES, BOOK 1

Tricia sat in her childhood home and gazed at the wall. Today had been particularly trying. In addition to flying from Seattle to Dallas, she had immediately started to take care of her mother. Diagnosed with Alzheimer's, her mother also had a heart condition, and like always, had refused to take any medicine.

Before she had moved to Texas, her mother had lived in Alabama where she saw the effects of the Tuskegee Experiment that lasted long after the experiment had officially ended. African-American men who were diagnosed with syphilis in the 1930s were tracked for forty years to see the long-term effects of the disease. Even when a cure came out in the 1950s, the doctors had not cured the men. Instead, they told patients who wanted to be treated that they had already been given medicine. Hundreds and thousands of people from the families were infected and affected by the trial.

Due to this, Tricia's mother refused to listen to white doctors. The crotchety old woman refused to believe that medicine would help or that anything was wrong with her. After an hour of trying and failing to convince her mother to take the medicine, Tricia had finally given up. She had made some bread pudding with dinner and sprinkled crumbled tablets into her mother's portions. It may not have been the most honest solution, but it worked. Now, Tricia was just exhausted.

Moving back to the kitchen, she started to make herself a cup of chamomile tea. With her mother in bed, it was time to drink some tea and unwind. Thankfully, she only had another two days until the weekend. Her brother Tyrone had promised to take care of her mother over the weekend so that Tricia could take a break and catch up with some old friends.

Sipping her cup of tea, she went to the bathroom and turned on the bathwater. As bubbles and warm water filled the tub, she slowly began to remove her clothes. Only a few days ago, she had left John. After telling him of her decision to return home to her mother, she had not talked to him or seen him again. Their brief fling had been as passionate as it was short-lived. She had taken care of his wife during the final stages of ALS. Although they had tried to stop their sexual desires from taking over, John and Tricia had made love more than a couple of times.

It was wrong and she still felt guilty. Despite her ethical concerns, she found herself wishing that she was still with him. His confident nature and unwavering conscience had attracted her to him from the moment they met.

Easing herself into the water, Tricia laughed to herself. If only her mother knew that she had slept with a rich, white man. She would never forgive her. Tricia picked up Jane Eyre and tried to read, but even her favorite novel could not distract her mind. She wanted John more than anything. It was impossible for her to go without sex anymore.

After realizing how fulfilling and satisfying sex could be with him, she was not willing to go back to her normal celibate lifestyle. She glanced at the bathroom door and saw that it was locked. Moving her hand down her body, she closed her eyes and pretended that her hand was John's. Tricia ran her fingertips around the dark cocoa-colored skin around her nipples and then drew it down further.

Initially, she started playing with the soft lips around her clit. This was not enough to satisfy her for long. She moved her clit in slow circles as she imagined John entering her for the first time in the office. The sex had been so magnetic, so electrically charged. She imagined his hard muscles moving against her and moaned.

The moan startled her. She looked at the door to see if her mother had heard anything. There were no sounds from the rest of the house. Moving her hand down along her body again, she moved her fingers faster and faster. Tricia could feel herself approaching orgasm when a sudden sound surprised her.

The shrill ringing of the phone pierced the air. For a moment, Tricia thought about ignoring it and finishing herself off. With a belabored sigh, she stood up and grabbed a towel. It could be someone important for her mother.

Exiting the bathroom, she rushed to reach the phone before it stopped ringing. "Hello?" she said with a breathy voice…

To purchase this book, look for **Love Anew by Shyla Starr.**

Also by this Author:

The Wife Swap

In Love with a Cougar

Stella for Christmas

The Long Ride Home

A Shot at Love

My Swedish Greta

The Second Honeymoon

Candy's Playmate

Sara's House of Hands

Loving My Sitter

His Wife and Her Husband

Bi-Curious Couple

Take Three, Mr. Writer

About the Author

Jack Ryder LOVES everything there is about sex!

When he is not involved with his "swinger" friends, enjoying a steamy threesome, or being part of a raunchy "gang bang", you can find him on first class planes, trains, and cruise ships. Traveling seems to be the BEST way to finding new and interesting sexmates for him. Sexmates. Plural. He lives with the saying "The More, The Merrier!"

He owns a successful business in New York. He writes as a hobby and also as sort of documentation of his mind-blowing sexcapades over the years. He is presently roaming around the streets of Manhattan but can be anywhere in the world too, since he travels often. So, beware! You just might be his next mate.

*"The most fun thing I enjoy when writing my stories is trying to figure out which is fantasy and which was memory. ENJOY! (Preferably with a friend. *wink*)" -Jack Ryder-*

From the Author

If you have any comments, suggestions, or would just like to get a little personal, please feel free to email me at:
jack_ryder@awesomeauthors.org

If you enjoyed any of my books then please share the love and click like on my books in Amazon.

If you write me a review and send me an email I will send you a free book, or many.
(Just know that these emails are filtered by my publisher.)

Good news is always welcome.

One Last Thing, For Kindle Readers...

When you turn the page, Kindle will give you the opportunity to rate this book and share your thoughts on Facebook and Twitter. If you enjoyed my writings, would you please take a few seconds to let your friends know about it? Because... when they enjoy they will be grateful to you and so will I.

Thank You!

Jack Ryder
jack_ryder@awesomeauthors.org

www.ingramcontent.com/pod-product-compliance
Lightning Source LLC
Chambersburg PA
CBHW071349130626
46556CB00005B/2099

* 9 7 8 1 6 8 0 3 0 0 5 2 9 *